THE FIRST CHRISTMAS PRESENTS

WHEN YOU were born, you were a little baby. I was a little baby once. Everybody was. When Jesus was born, He was a little baby, too. But He was not a common ordinary baby. He came down from Heaven to live with us in our world. His Father was God.

JESUS HAD a very good Mother who loved Him very much. Her name was Mary. Her husband was Good Saint Joseph. Jesus was not born at home, in the house of Mary and Joseph. He was born when they were on a trip, in a little town that was called Bethlehem.

JESUS WAS born on Christmas. That is His birthday. There was no room in the hotel, so Mary and Joseph had to stay in a cave that was used as a stable for horses and cows. There was nothing but a manger for the Baby to lie in. (A manger is a big feeding box for the animals.) Blessed Mother wrapped her Baby up to keep Him warm. Saint Joseph put some nice clean straw in the manger for Him to lie on. Then they both kissed Him.

DURING the night when Jesus was born, and everything was very quiet, there were some shepherds in a field outside of Bethlehem. They were watching their sheep, to keep away wolves and thieves. All of a sudden, many Angels came from Heaven. They told the shepherds, "Go over to Bethlehem and see God's Son. He was born tonight. You will find Him all wrapped up, lying in a manger." Then the Angels flew back to Heaven, singing lovely songs.

THE SHEPHERDS ran up to Bethlehem to see the Baby Jesus. Of course, they brought Him birthday presents. One shepherd brought a little white lamb. He knelt down and said, "Holy Child, I have brought You a present." One shepherd brought a little coal-black kid goat with long silky ears. He knelt down and said, "Holy Child, I have brought You a present." Other shepherds brought milk and woolly sheepskins to keep the Baby warm.

GOD PUT a bright new star in the sky the night His Son was born. Far, far away, three Wise Men saw the star. They were very good men, so God let them know what the star meant. They got on their camels and came riding, riding, a long, long way to find Jesus.

THE STAR pointed to the place where Jesus and Mary and Joseph were. The Wise Men followed it. They found the Baby. They knew that He was God's Son, and so they knelt down and bowed low. They talked to the Holy Child and told Him they loved Him. They all gave Him presents, money and expensive things. The first one kissed one of His little hands. The second one kissed both of His little hands. The third one kissed His little feet.

WOULD YOU like to give a present to Jesus too? What Jesus wants from children is their love. He wants all the children in the world to love Him. Jesus said, "Give Me your heart." He wants you to tell Him you love Him.

NOW FOLD your hands and close your eyes. Pretend you are in the cave with Jesus and Mary and Joseph. Whisper to Baby Jesus:

"I want to give You a present. I give You my heart. I love You. Teach me how to love You more every day."

BABY BUNTING FROM A HANDKERCHIEF

A baby bunting is quickly made from one of Daddy's large handkerchiefs.
Tie a knot in one corner of the handkerchief. This is the head, with a little pointed cap on it.
Now gather up a little material on either side of the knot, to shape the arms.

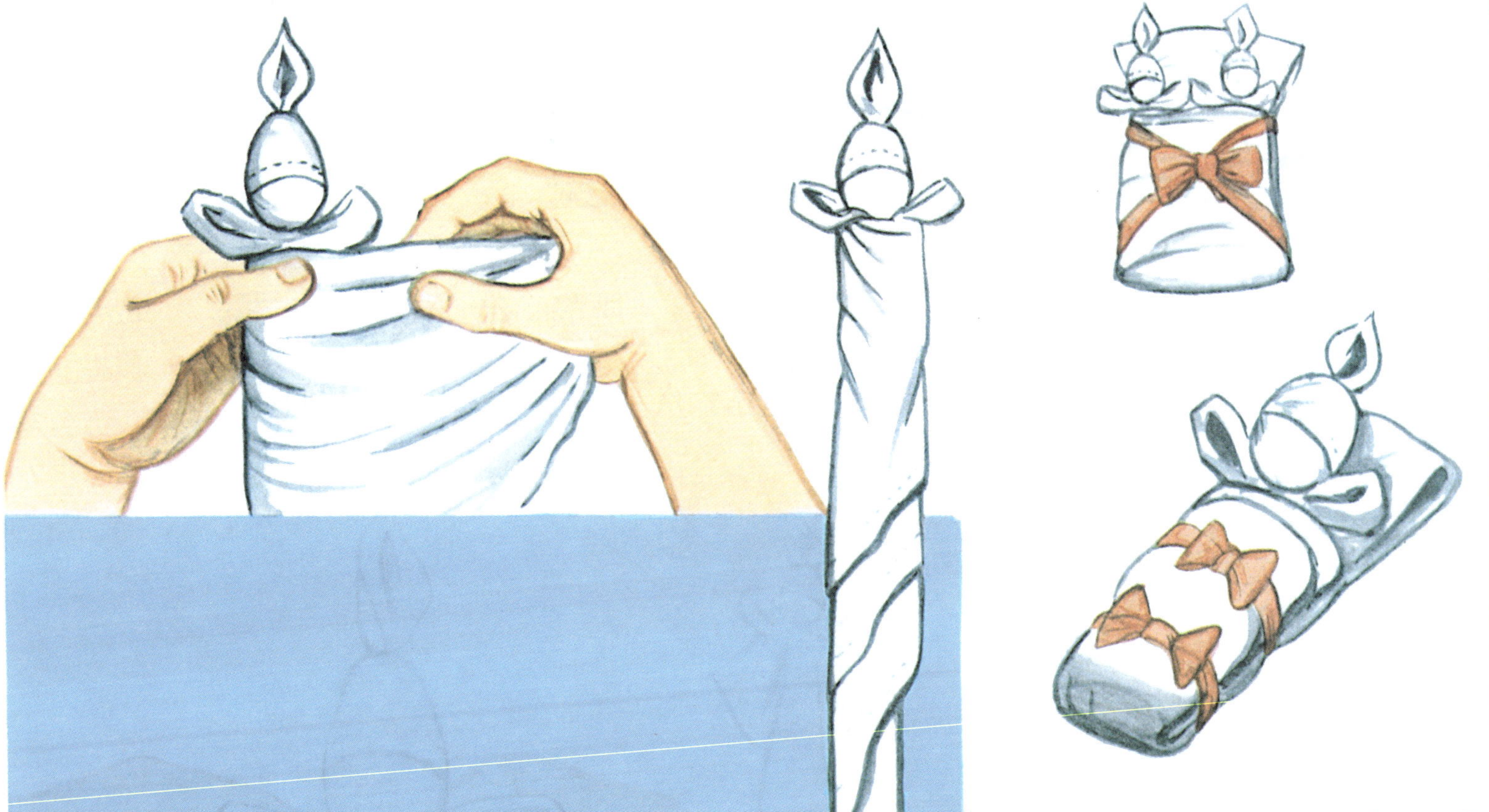

Use only half of the material between the head and the next corners and use what is left to wrap around the body, keeping the arms in place.

The "body" now will be one long roll. Fold it over twice in back–and there will be your baby in its bunting! If you tie it together with a ribbon, it will look prettier and will last longer.

People with very nimble fingers can even make twins, by using two corners next to each other for the heads and using only very little material for the four arms.

THE SPOTTED DEVIL

Lots of things had been happening at Matongu. Just one week after Father George got there, Father Christopher and Brother William of St. Amadeus arrived to help him. Father Christopher had been in Africa for a long time. He had a long white beard and twinkly blue eyes and the children just loved him. Father George put him in charge of teaching the children about God.

Brother Bill, which is what Brother William of St. Amadeus was called for short, was a great big man with a reddish beard. He could do almost anything and was very busy getting ready to build a house and chapel. Great trees had been cut down and were lying neatly trimmed by the hut. Down by the stream, strong men were digging clay to be used for making bricks. It would not be long before the house and chapel were built.

Sunny John and his friend Ngomi were helping Brother Bill. They carried bricks for him and put them neatly in a pile. Their mothers, Ntaka-Ntaka and Mulaya, were talking to each other as they watched the children.

"After all," said Mulaya to Ntaka-Ntaka, "they have the rest of their lives to build a house. What are they rushing around for? And anyway, what's wrong with the hut? Old Kalabi has lived in a hut since the great trees of the forest were saplings, and he's none the worse for it, is he?"

Father George did not feel the same way about his hut. He was tired of beetles and spiders dropping on his bed at night, and he did not like the snakes that crawled out of the grass roof and hid under his pillow. Father George was looking forward to the new house that would not have all these surprises.

Brother Bill was hard at work making stacks of bricks, and the children would help for a while and then forget to help and get in the way. Brother Bill would frown ferociously and they would pretend to be scared and run away. But Brother Bill could not be ferocious for very long, so they would come back and do a little more helping. Sunny was there almost all the time with his friends Ngomi and Monguli and Bakra. They all loved Brother Bill and the wonderful toys he made for them out of clay.

Wupsy had not been very busy lately. He had frightened those devils all the way to Upper Egypt and hardly any of them had come back. But he knew that it took more than that to stop a devil for long, and Wupsy had been noticing signs of trouble. He had been warned to "Keep a sharp lookout for strange devils!" He had not forgotten and was expecting things to happen any minute.

One afternoon Wupsy was singing hymns to the Queen of the Angels because the tree he had chosen for a lookout post was covered with blue flowers and they reminded him of her. Sunny was down below building a wall of bricks, and he had his back to a great pile of bricks from which he took one every now and again. Brother Bill had gone off to say his Rosary, and the workers were taking it easy, as they usually did when Brother Bill was not around.

Suddenly Wupsy stopped singing and listened very carefully. What was that horrible rattling noise? It sounded just like a devil.

Yes, there it was again. It was a devil noise. And then Wupsy saw him. This devil was new to Wupsy, a devil he had never seen before. What could he be up to? Wupsy watched carefully. The devil was behind the great pile of bricks. This Wupsy knew just as clearly as if the devil had told him. He was pushing the pile of bricks with all his might so they would fall on Sunny!

This was awful! At first Wupsy was going to fly down and chase the devil away. Then he decided it would be more fun to have a push-of-war with this devil. So he flew down quietly to the other side of the bricks and did some pushing too. The devil pushed and pushed until he was sore all over, but the bricks did not budge one inch. He could not figure out why the bricks would not move.

The devil hobbled to the end of the pile and peeked around to the other side. He got the shock of his life! He came face to face with Wupsy, who was laughing hard. Devils just hate to be laughed at, but to be laughed at by an Angel who had just won a battle with him was too much. The devil slunk off as quickly as he could. He knew where there was a nice dirty bog in the forest where he had lots of slimy friends, and where he knew there would be no Angels.

Wupsy saw him safely out of the village, and then flew back to his tree with the blue flowers to think things over. This was serious. Why should a special devil come all the way from you-know-where to push a pile of bricks down on top of Sunny John? The devils must realize that Sunny was rather special. Maybe they even guessed the plans that God had for him. Wupsy shivered at the thought. He would have to be even more careful!

THE DIFFERENCE IS:
A eats more than a .
A is taller than a .
A is harder than a .
My are lower than my .
4 apples are more than 2.
A is younger than U.
A runs faster than a .
are better than a .
A is cooler than a .
A gives more milk than a .
A is sweeter than a .
And maybe U are smarter than .
CAKE
U YOU
COW
2 TWO
GOAT
I
DRESS
TOY
MOUSE
PLAYMATES
PIE
CAR
CHURCH
BED
COAT
HEAD
BABY
HOUSE
FEET
DOG
4 FOUR
BENCH
U YOU
BOY

THE SECRET

One day Danny Dinkel wandered into the garden of his next-door neighbor and looked into the kitchen where Mrs. Squibble was working busily.

"Good morning, Mrs. Squibble," he said politely and inhaled with satisfaction the delicious smell of baking cookies.

When he got no answer to his greeting, he tried again: "Why does it smell like cookies?" He was used to having long chats with Mrs. Squibble. This morning, however, she only looked up briefly from her work.

"Because I'm baking cookies, Danny! Run along now, I'm very rushed today."

Danny never gave up easily. "Why are you making cookies?" he asked. But Mrs. Squibble did not feel like playing a long game of questions and answers.

"Because the King and Queen of Ask-Me-Not are coming for tea at four o'clock. Now, run along!"

Her voice sounded so firm that Danny decided to leave. He was halfway through the garden gate when Mrs. Squibble called him. Hopefully, he returned to the kitchen door.

"Why did you call, Mrs. Squibble?"

"Because the first cookies are ready. Here, have one. And, by the way, what I told you about the King and Queen is a secret," she added, with a twinkle in her eye.

Danny shuffled away, munching the cookie. He had not gone far when he met Betsy from across the street.

"Where did you get that cookie, Danny?"

"It's a secret," Danny answered. But Betsy said she wouldn't breathe a word.

"Mrs. Squibble gave it to me. She's expecting the King and Queen of Ask-Me-Not for tea at four o'clock. That's why she's making cookies."

Betsy was delighted with the news. She skipped along the street, chanting happily: "Nobody knows what I know! Nobody knows what I know!"

"What do you know?" asked Ann, who was on her way to do some shopping.

"I can't tell you. It's a secret."

"Surely you can tell your best friend!"

"No, I can't. Danny said Mrs. Squibble told him it was a secret."

"I won't tell anybody you told me," pleaded Ann. "I can keep a secret."

"Are you sure?"

"I'm sure. What is it?"

"The Squibbles are expecting the King and Queen of Ask-Me-Not for tea at four o'clock. That's why Mrs. Squibble is making cookies."

Betsy skipped along and entered the store. There she met Bill.

"You are looking mighty pleased," Bill observed when he saw her.

"Oh, I'm just thinking of something I heard."

"Well, what did you hear?"

"It's a secret. Betsy said that Danny told her Mrs. Squibble didn't want anybody to know about it."

"Pah! I'm not interested in your silly secret," scoffed Bill.

Bill was almost two years older and Ann felt hurt.

"It isn't silly. If you won't tell anybody, I'll whisper it in your ear."

That afternoon at four o'clock, Mrs. Squibble heard a great commotion in front of her house. She opened the door to see what was the matter. Imagine her surprise when she saw a large group of boys and girls gathered there, all dressed in their Sunday best.

"Whatever has gotten into you?" she exclaimed. "What do you want?"

"We want to see the King and Queen of Ask-Me-Not!" shouted the children.

Mrs. Squibble sat down on her doorstep and laughed so hard that the tears rolled down her cheeks.

"Dear, dear!" she panted when she had recovered her breath. "However did you hear about them?"

"Sam told me–Jack said–Susan told him that Jack had said to her–Emily knew that Bill had said to Pete–Ann told him–that Betsy said–Danny had told her you didn't want anybody to know that you baked cookies for the King and Queen of Ask-Me-Not!" said a little girl standing nearest to her.

"So that's it!" laughed Mrs. Squibble. "My, my—secrets certainly do travel fast around here!"

When she noticed all the little faces in front of her turn red as beets, she reached for the cookie jar on the table behind her.

"The King and Queen of Ask-Me-Not were not able to come," she said with a twinkle in her eye. "But since you have come all the way to see them, it is only fair that you should sample the cookies they did not eat."

And that is just what they did.